# DEEP TROUBLE AT DOLPHIN BAY

## M. D. Spenser

Paradise Press, Inc.

**Weston, FL**

32124-2

S0-BNG-867

Published by Paradise Press, Inc. by arrangement with River Publishing, Inc. All
right, title and interest to the "HUMANOMORPHS" logo and design are owned by
River Publishing, Inc. No portion of the "HUMANOMORPHS" logo and design
may be reproduced in part or whole without prior written permission from River
Publishing, Inc. An application for a registered trademark of the "HUMANO-
MORPHS" logo and design is pending with the Federal Patent and Trademark
office.

ISBN 1-57657-338-9

EXCLUSIVE DISTRIBUTION BY PARADISE PRESS, INC.

Cover Design by & Illustrations by Nicholas Forder

Printed in the U.S.A.

To Travis and Gail, with love.

# **<u>Chapter One</u>**

If Derrick Granger hadn't been staring at the strange boat, he might not have stumbled into trouble that day.

But as he walked along the beach he couldn't take his eyes from the sleek vessel. It seemed to hover like a giant bat just above the waves, far out in the bay.

He had never seen anything like it. It looked like it should be flying through space, not floating on the sea.

It was long, low and black, and its broad, curved bow seemed split in half, as if it had two separate hulls. Two round satellite dishes rose like giant bat ears from the top of the windowless cabin.

Even though it was far out in the bay, he could tell it was big — much bigger than the sailboats he usually saw bobbing in the waves.

Derrick couldn't take his eyes from it. He pulled off his thick glasses — he was very nearsighted

1

— and wiped the lenses to get a better view.

Ordinarily when he walked on the beach, he wasn't interested in what was floating on top of the water. He worried about the creatures hidden beneath it.

Creatures that secretly watched him, hungrily following his every move, just waiting for him to step too close to the water.

Derrick's father said he was being silly. His father was a marine scientist who studied dolphins and other ocean creatures. Derrick lived in North Carolina. But he was spending the summer with his dad at Dolphin Bay, a little town in the Florida Keys where his dad conducted ocean research.

His dad loved the ocean. Sometimes he spent hours swimming underwater with an air tank and a mask, studying fish and mollusks and coral reefs. He said it was a different world underwater, just like in outer space. If Derrick would learn more about sea creatures, his dad said, he wouldn't be so afraid of them.

"Sure, Dad," Derrick would say, rolling his eyes as he imagined himself being skewered by a swordfish.

Derrick wasn't tall and athletic like his father. He was a short chubby ten year old with bad eyes and a buzz haircut who sunburned easily and couldn't swim. He was afraid of the water, and even more afraid of the creatures living in it.

Creatures like huge lobsters with long painful pincers. Or jellyfish with poisonous stinging tentacles.

Or octopuses just waiting to wrap him in their deadly embrace. Or — worst of all — torpedo-shaped sharks with smiles full of jagged teeth.

OK, Derrick had to admit that it was unlikely he was going to be attacked by a shark while strolling on the beach. After all, he always stayed at least three feet from the water. But then, he had heard of something called a "walking catfish" that could actually move across dry land.

If you could have a walking catfish, why not a walking shark? Or — even worse — a *running* shark?

Mother Nature was mischievous. You never knew what she might send your way.

When he went camping with the Boy Scouts, a rainstorm caused the tent to collapse on his head like a soggy pancake. When he decided to take up insect collecting, a bee stung him on the tongue. And when he went wading in the creek, she sent a crawdad to bite his big toe.

That was why Derrick didn't care much for the ocean or any other part of nature. He liked indoor activities, like eating, reading Greek mythology and listening to "Clueless Hairballs" CDs.

They were his favorite band. He even had six "Clueless Hairballs" T-shirts, one of which he was wearing now.

His eyes shifted back to the ship on the horizon.

Wow.

From that angle, it sort of resembled a giant stingray, waiting for its prey.

Keeping his eyes on the ship, Derrick moved a step farther away from the water.

"Watch out!" someone shouted.

As Derrick whirled towards the voice, something raked across his shins. Giant jaws seemed to close around his right leg.

He screamed as he fell towards the water.

"Help me!" he shouted.

He clawed at the sand. A wave washed over him, filling his nose and eyes with warm, salty water.

The water stung his eyes, temporarily blinding him. He couldn't see what held his leg. But its grip was tightening.

He imagined himself being dragged out to sea.

"Help me!" he sputtered, coughing and gasping for air. "Please, someone help me!"

# Chapter Two

"Stop flopping around like a flounder, and I'll get it off of you."

At the sound of the voice, Derrick became very still. It was the voice of a young girl. She didn't seem the least bit concerned that his leg had become shark bait.

In fact, she sounded angry.

Derrick patted the sand around his head and finally found his glasses. Just as he put them on, his leg slipped free from the jaws that had held it.

He looked up and saw a red-haired girl about his own age inspecting a bent beach chair.

"Congratulations," she said sarcastically. "You've ruined my chair. Why don't you watch where you're going?"

Sitting in the wet sand, Derrick looked dumbly from the girl to the chair to his leg. There was a red scrape just above his ankle. As he rubbed the tender skin, he realized what had happened.

When he stumbled against the metal chair frame, his foot had gotten lodged in the hinged joint. As the chair closed, it had pinched his skin.

Great.

He had been attacked by a beach chair.

Derrick turned as red as a boiled lobster. Something like this would never happen to Hercules.

"I-I'm sorry," he managed to stammer. "I didn't see it."

The girl looked him over with cool green eyes. She was almost as tall as Derrick, and her skin was as brown as a coconut. Derrick was suddenly aware of his pale legs and arms. He thought of how pudgy and white his belly looked under his baggy "Clueless Hairballs" T-shirt.

"You're not from around here, are you?" the girl asked.

Derrick shook his head.

"No. Just visiting for the summer. My dad runs the dolphin research center."

The girl's eyes widened.

"Your dad is Edward Granger, the marine researcher?"

Derrick nodded, steeling himself for another lash of sarcasm.

"Wow," the girl gasped. "That's so neat. I've

read about the experiments he's doing to find out how dolphins communicate."

She laid down the chair and held out her hand.

"I'm Kerri," she said as they shook hands. "Kerri Sanders. I live on the other side of the bay but I come over here almost every day to look for shells. That's what I was doing when you trashed my chair."

She held up a bulging mesh bag.

"See? I found all these this afternoon. You wouldn't believe all the different kinds — look, I even found a moon shell."

"Ummm. Very nice," Derrick said, trying to seem interested.

"You can have it," Kerri said, putting the small, pink shell in his hand. "I've lots more."

Derrick shoved it into his pocket. He hoped it didn't still have a snail in it.

"Hey," Kerri suddenly said. "You want to go swimming?"

"No, I don't think so. I . . . I . . . " Derrick started to tell her that he couldn't swim, then hesitated. "I just ate a big lunch. I probably shouldn't go into the water."

He didn't like to lie. But he didn't feel like being laughed at again either.

Kerri seemed disappointed.

7

"How about a walk then?" she said. "I want to know more about your dad."

"Okay," Derrick said. "But not too fast. I think I twisted my ankle when I fell over your chair."

Kerri giggled.

"You really did look funny flopping around on the sand," she said.

Derrick's face began turning red.

"Look, I said I'm sorry about your chair," he said. "I didn't see it because I was looking at that weird boat."

Kerri looked puzzled.

"What boat?"

"You know — the big black boat. Out there."

Derrick pointed across the bay.

But the boat wasn't there. There was only a little blue sailboat, bobbing on the waves like a bath toy.

"It was there just a minute ago," Derrick said, his eyes searching the horizon. "Honest, it was there. I saw it."

Kerri laughed.

"Maybe we should go sit in the shade," she said. "I think you've been out in the sun too long."

# **<u>Chapter Three</u>**

Derrick watched the three dolphins swimming lazily around the big pool at the research center.

They were in their usual formation. Flash, the big male dolphin, was in the middle, flanked on either side by the females Dorie and Belle.

Derrick had little interest in dolphins or his father's work, but sometimes he enjoyed watching them frolic in the water. They were so sleek and graceful. They surfaced and dove as if waltzing on water.

If I could learn to swim like that, Derrick thought, I'd probably like the ocean a lot more.

Although his father sometimes put on a rubber suit and went into the pool with the dolphins, Derrick knew they were not simply large playful puppies. His father had told him that dolphins could be territorial and aggressive.

And while their sharp white teeth weren't as menacing as a shark's, dolphins were fierce fighters when they needed to be. They could break bones with a flip of their tail, or crush a shark's chest by ramming it with their hard beaks.

Flash had a big scar on his back where he had once tangled with a shark. That's how he had ended up in the research project. Fishermen had found the bottle-nosed dolphin battered and bleeding off the coast of South Florida.

After many months, he had finally been nursed back to health. Eventually, he had been donated to the research center, just like Dorie and Belle.

Derrick sighed and looked at his watch.

Almost one o'clock.

Where was Kerri?

She was half an hour late. She was supposed to meet him at the center so he could show her the dolphins and introduce her to his father. Then they were going to the beach to fly kites.

He was looking forward to seeing Kerri again, too. Since bumping into her last week, he had met her almost every day at the beach.

Sometime they went for long walks, searching for shells. Sometimes they built big, complicated sandcastles and fortresses.

Sometimes they just sat on the sand and talked.

Kerri told him how bored she was in school

and how much she loved the ocean and being out-doors. Derrick told her about mythic figures like Zeus, the god from Greek mythology who could summon thunderbolts from heaven, and Medusa, who had a headful of snakes.

"I'd hate to cut *her* hair," Kerri laughed.

Kerri joked around a lot. She liked to throw water on him and slip up behind him when he wasn't looking. That was one of the things he liked about her. His father was so serious all the time, thinking about his work, but Kerri was always playing jokes.

She probably would just make a joke if he told her he couldn't swim.

Derrick had come close to telling her a couple of times. But something — a nagging fear of what she might say — always silenced him. Whenever Kerri suggested they go into the water, Derrick had to make up an excuse to stay on the beach.

He looked at his watch again. Almost 1:15.

Where was she?

Just then his father emerged from the little of-fice where he spent hours each day studying computer charts and tinkering with electrical devices. He walked over to Derrick.

"It's almost feeding time," he said. "I thought your friend would be here by now."

"Me, too. I don't know where she is," Derrick said. "Want me to help bring in the fish?"

"No, Boris can help me. I'll go find him."

Boris was his father's new assistant at the center. He was a tall, muscular man with a gleaming, shaved head and small black eyes that rarely seemed to blink.

Jeff, his father's previous assistant, had been talkative and friendly. But Boris rarely spoke.

More than once, Derrick had felt Boris glumly watching him. It was like being watched by a gorilla, because Boris usually had a banana in his hand. The dude must eat a case of bananas a day, Derrick thought.

Derrick's dad sometimes scolded Boris for tossing his banana peels into the bay. Otherwise, they seemed to get along fine. He said he was lucky that Boris had shown up at the center, looking for a job, only a day or so after Jeff had been paralyzed in the motorcycle accident.

Suddenly there was a thrashing in the pool, and a high-pitched, stuttering squeal.

For a moment, Derrick thought Kerri had snuck into the center and jumped into the water. Then he realized it was Belle.

The dolphin, which had a bell-shaped white

patch on her side, had swum to the edge of the pool near where Derrick was standing. Belle seemed to be looking straight at him. She was making the chattering, laugh-like sounds that dolphins make when they're in a playful mood.

It's almost like she's smiling at me, Derrick thought.

He moved a few steps closer to the pool.

The dolphin wagged its head and seemed to laugh again.

Derrick moved a few steps closer.

"Are you wanting to play, girl?" he softly asked.

He was at the edge of the pool now, so close that he could actually look into the dolphin's reddish-brown eyes. He could see the texture of her sleek gray skin.

Slowly, he extended his hand. He had never touched a dolphin before.

As the hand approached, Belle rolled onto her side. She was like a puppy waiting to be scratched on the belly.

"Well, aren't you friendly," Derrick said.

Then, with his hand inches from the dolphin's white stomach, he stopped.

Something had moved behind him.

Before he could turn to see what it was, two hands shoved hard against his back.

He didn't even have time to scream.

For one terrifying moment, he seemed to be suspended over the edge of the pool, looking into the dolphin's eyes.

Then black fear enfolded him, and the water closed over his head.

## Chapter Four

When he felt the first shock of cold water, Derrick began thrashing his arms and legs.

He wasn't trying to swim. He was just trying to keep from sinking.

But it wasn't working. He kept bobbing under the water. He was trying to hold his breath, but his lungs were already starting to burn. He would have to take a breath soon.

And if he tried to breathe underwater, it would be the last breath he ever took.

Suddenly, as he batted his arms around in the water, he felt his head burst above the surface. He gasped for air and tried to shout.

Miraculously, his glasses had stayed on his face, although they were perched precariously on his nose. Frantically, he looked around the pool, searching for whoever had shoved him off.

Even as panicky and terrified as he was — he couldn't believe what he saw.

15

Kerri was standing at the edge of the pool.

Looking down at him, laughing.

How could she be laughing, he thought. Couldn't she see that he was drowning?

He made a strangled attempt to cry out, but water went down his throat and he began coughing. He made another desperate attempt to call out. Then he felt himself sinking into the cold water again.

He was completely under the water again now, thrashing about violently. The water was so cold. His lungs were burning again.

I can't hold my breath any longer, Derrick thought. I've got to breathe.

He wasn't sure what happened after that. Later, he just remembered feeling something bump hard against his body, and a big piece of plastic seemed to slide against his hand and arm.

Instinctively, he grabbed it. As his arm curled around it, he felt himself pulled up through the water as if a powerful boat was towing him.

A second later, his head broke through the surface.

He took a huge, shuddering breath, desperately holding onto the piece of plastic that had saved his life.

Only it wasn't a piece of plastic.

It was a fin.

A big shiny dolphin dorsal fin, sticking up from a scarred back. Somehow, he managed to hold on, and Flash towed him to the little metal ladder at the end of the pool.

"What happened? It looked like you had forgotten how to swim."

Kerri's anxious face peered down at him as he sat panting at the edge of the pool.

"I didn't forget," Derrick said.

"Then what happened? I thought you were just playing, but then it looked like you were really in trouble until the dolphin found you. What happened?"

Before Derrick could answer, his father and Boris appeared beside them, holding a big bucket of cold fish.

"Derrick, are you all right?" his father asked, an anxious frown on his face. "How did you get wet?"

Derrick glanced at Kerri, whose face was suddenly drained of color. His father didn't allow horseplay around the dolphins. If his dad knew that Kerri had pushed him into the pool, he might ban her from the center.

"I slipped on some water," he said. "I just got a little too close. But I was able to grab the ladder. I'm OK."

His father shook his head.

"You've got to be extra careful around the pool. Either that, or wear a life jacket."

He picked up the bucket and went over to the feeding platform, a small wooden deck a few feet above the water.

"You're just lucky Flash didn't think you were trying to take over his territory," his father said. "You could have been seriously hurt."

Derrick nodded, not wanting to look at Kerri.

"Let's get these dolphins fed, Boris," his father said.

Boris bent to pick up the heavy bucket — but not before his eyes met Derrick's, and a smirking smile briefly bent his lips.

After they had dropped dozens of herring and smelt into the churning water, Mr. Granger asked Kerri and Derrick whether they would like to see his new dolphin-signaling device. He went into his office and came back with a laptop computer, connected to a strange-looking microphone on a long cord.

"This is a called a hydrophone," he said. "It's basically a microphone that works underwater."

He went to the far end of the pool and lowered the hydrophone into the water.

"Boris, get them to follow you to the other end

of the pool," he said.

The assistant went to the other end of the pool. As he made quick, flicking motion with his arm, as if he were throwing out food, the dolphins swam towards him.

They waited in the water, squealing and clicking.

"Now watch what happens when I give them the signal," Mr. Granger said.

He tapped a few computer keys. Immediately, the dolphins turned and zoomed towards him. He rewarded each of them with another fish.

"That's amazing," Kerri said. "How did you do it?"

"The hydrophone broadcasts a special high-frequency underwater signal," Mr. Granger said. "I've trained the dolphins to respond differently as I vary the frequency. Watch this."

He tapped again on the keyboard. The dolphins suddenly darted back towards Boris.

"Wow," Kerri said. "How many different commands can you give them?"

"Right now, only about a half dozen, but I hope eventually to be able to train them to respond to many different signals."

Kerri watched the dolphins gliding in front of

Boris.

"How far away can they hear the signal?" she asked.

"This one has a range of twenty miles or so," Mr. Grange said. "But I've almost finished a much stronger transmitter that should communicate with them from at least a thousand miles away."

"Amazing," Kerri said. "It's almost like an underwater remote control."

Mr. Granger pulled the hydrophone from the water.

"Well, I have to get back to work," he said. "Are you kids going back to the beach?"

"We're going to fly kites," Derrick said.

"Have fun — don't get too near the water."

Derrick saw a puzzled look cross Kerri's face. He pulled her towards the door.

"Huh?" she said. "Don't go near the water. Who did he mean by that?"

"Who knows," Derrick said. "Maybe he's afraid I'll be attacked by another beach chair."

# **Chapter Five**

The next day, Derrick was lying on the bed reading when the phone rang.

He was rereading the story of Medusa, the Gorgon whose hair had been turned into a snarl of hissing snakes. Anyone who looked at her immediately turned to stone.

But Perseus, the son of the Greek God Zeus, had chopped off her head by using his shiny shield as a mirror so he didn't have to look at her. That Perseus was a clever dude, Derrick thought as he went into the kitchen to answer the phone.

It was Kerri. She invited him over for dinner at her house that evening.

"Sounds like fun," Derrick said. "I'll have to ask my dad, but I'm sure it'll be OK with him."

It was a hot, sunny day and he had carried the cordless phone out onto the patio as he talked to Kerri. He sat down on a metal chair beneath the big patio umbrella.

He had just started to dial his dad's office when he realized he hadn't asked Kerri what time dinner would be. He dialed her number.

It rang once. Twice. Three times. Then someone picked up.

He heard a faint hello, as if someone were speaking through a long pipe. Then there was a crash of static, followed by scratchy screeches and weird whistles.

"Hello? Kerri?"

More static. More screeches.

Just as Derrick was about to hang up, he heard a voice.

But it wasn't Kerri.

The voice was deep and gruff, as if it were rumbling up out of a barrel.

" . . . usually goes home about seven o'clock in the evening," the voice was saying. "We'll wait a couple of hours and then make our move."

Derrick was about to hang up when he heard another voice, this one as soft and whispery as surf on sand.

"And you're sure there won't be a night watchman or security guard? We can't afford to be discovered before we get the dolphins. It would blow the whole plan."

"No guards," the gruff voice replied. "It'll be like breaking into a doughnut shop. Swift and sweet. There's only one alarm, and our man inside will pull the plug on that."

There was a soft, whispery laugh.

"Like a doughnut shop, huh? You're making me hungry, Charlie. So, how long you think the gig will take?"

"A couple of hours. It'll take a while to load the dolphins. But by this time tomorrow, we'll be a thousand miles at sea, getting ready to spring our little surprise party on the world."

Another whispery laugh.

"Yeah, our little party," the soft voice chuckled. "It should be a real blast. A billion dollar blast."

There was another crackle of static. The line went dead.

Derrick stood holding the phone in his hand.

The sun was hot and bright. But a cold tremor of fear shot through him, and he felt as if he had again fallen into deep, dangerous waters.

# Chapter Six

Derrick stood absolutely still in the hot sun, his eyes large and unblinking behind the thick glasses.

He didn't want to believe what he had overheard on the phone.

But his ears hadn't deceived him. Someone was plotting to kidnap his dad's dolphins. And they were going to do it that very night.

He sank down into one of the metal chairs on the patio, then jumped up as the hot metal burned the back of his legs. The flash of pain seemed to kick his brain back into action.

He had to warn his father.

His hand shook as he dialed the research center.

Thankfully, there was no static this time. But there wasn't an answer, either. Just a busy signal.

Heaving a deep sigh, Derrick cut off the phone. Now what?

Maybe he should call the police. But would

they believe his story? He wasn't even sure *he* believed it.

Maybe he should call Kerri. But what could she do?

Impatiently, he picked up the phone and dialed the research center again.

Beep. Beep. Beep.

Frustrated, Derrick banged down the phone. He couldn't sit around waiting.

The research center was only a couple of miles away. By the time the phone line was free, he could be halfway there, he thought.

He took the phone back into the kitchen and sprinted out the door.

Derrick ran almost all the way to the research center. He zigzagged along several blocks of sidewalks, then turned onto a narrow beachfront lane that ran past rows of rusty warehouses and sagging docks. Finally, as he left the paved lane and ran down a curving, shell-paved drive, the center came into view.

The front door was open. Drenched in sweat and gasping for breath, he stumbled inside.

"Dad!" he shouted. "Where are you?"

His voice echoed through the cavernous building.

"Dad?"

His father wasn't there. The building was empty, except for Derrick and the dolphins.

Maybe he's out back on the dock, Derrick thought, sprinting for the rear door. But no one was there, either. Only a few white gulls hovering above the bay.

Then he noticed that his father's small skiff was gone

Derrick turned back towards the building.

He was almost to the door when a voice startled him.

"What are you doing here?" Boris demanded.

He stood in the doorway, muscular arms folded across his chest.

"I . . . I'm looking for my dad. I've got to talk to him."

Boris scowled.

"He took the boat out into the bay to do some equipment tests. He won't be back for several hours."

"I've got to talk to him," Derrick said, his voice rising in desperation. "It's an emergency."

Boris's eyes narrowed.

"What kind of emergency?"

Derrick hesitated. Boris probably wouldn't believe him. He might even make fun of him. But he had to tell someone.

"They're going to kidnap the dolphins," Derrick blurted out. "I heard them on the phone. They're coming to get the dolphins tonight."

Boris didn't laugh. His eyes widened, as if he had just seen an alien space ship, and his jaw clenched. Then he put a hand on Derrick's shoulder.

"Come inside," he said. "Tell me everything you heard."

Derrick followed him back into the building. Quickly, he repeated the phone conversation he had overheard. Boris listened intently, nodding thoughtfully from time to time.

"We've got to warn Dad," Derrick said.

"I've got an idea," Boris said. "I'll call the Shore Patrol. Maybe they can get a message to Mr. Granger."

Boris turned and went into the office where Derrick's father worked. As Derrick watched through the big glass window, Boris made the call.

Derrick couldn't hear what Boris was saying, but he spoke excitedly into the phone, gesturing with his hands. When he emerged from the office, he was smiling.

"The Shore Patrol will help," he said. "They're going to find your father and bring him back. Now I'm going to the police and tell them about the plot."

Derrick felt a sense of relief.

Boris believed him.

"I'll go with you," Derrick said. "The police may want to question me."

Boris hesitated, then shook his head.

"No," he said. "You'd better go back home. Your father will probably try to call you there."

Derrick nodded. He started towards the door. As he walked across the cement floor, he was startled to hear a high-pitched squeal. He looked towards the pool.

Flash seemed to be barking at him. Half of the dolphin's body was out of the water as it gave a quick series of high pipping squeals, shaking its head from side to side.

It's almost like he's trying to tell me something, Derrick thought as he watched the dolphin's agitated movements.

As Derrick looked into the dolphin's reddish eyes, he had an uncomfortable sense that the dolphin really was trying to warn him.

Then, telling himself he was being silly, Derrick turned and walked away.

# **Chapter Seven**

By the time he walked back to his father's house, Derrick was exhausted.

He collapsed onto the bed and pulled the cool pillow under his sweaty head. He felt drowsy. But whenever he closed his eyes, he saw the shadowy images of swimming men.

Two men dressed in wet suits, with big knives on their belts and spear guns in their hands. They swam slowly through murky water. They were looking for someone.

Him.

Derrick forced his eyes open. He thought back over the phone call. What did the kidnappers plan to do with the dolphins? What had the man meant by a billion-dollar blast?

The more Derrick went over it in his mind, the wearier he felt. His eyes closed again. . . .

The two men swam back into view. This time, one of them had a long cord tied to his hand. The cord disappeared into the murky water. Derrick could not see what was at the other end.

The two men looked to the right. Looked to the left.

They saw Derrick.

The man tugged on the cord. Derrick saw a dark shape looming out of the murky depths. It was a huge fish.

A dolphin on a leash, he thought.

Then the creature swam fully into view.

It wasn't a dolphin.

It was a great white shark, streaking towards him like a razor-toothed torpedo.

He tried to flee, then realized he could not swim.

The shark was closing fast. . . . Only feet away now.

Alarm bells sounded in his mind. . . . Shrill sirens of terror. . . . Screams. . . . Derrick's eyes flew open. The phone was ringing.

Dad! he thought. He ran to the kitchen.

"Hello," he said breathlessly. "Dad?"

"Derrick?" It was Kerri. "I thought you were going to call me back about dinner."

Dinner. In his panic over the intercepted phone call, he had forgotten about Kerri. He didn't want to disappoint her, but he had to talk to his father.

"I'm sorry," he said. "Something came up. I still haven't had a chance to ask my dad if it's OK."

"You sound strange, Derrick. Is something wrong?"

A part of Derrick wanted to confide in Kerri. He knew that she would believe him. She might even want to help him. He took a deep breath.

"There's something going on with the dolphins," he began. "Some men are planning . . . "

Derrick stopped. He thought he had heard a sound at the front door.

He peered into the living room and saw his father walking into the house.

"I'll call you back," he told Kerri and hurriedly hung up.

"Dad!" he burst out. "They're going to kidnap the dolphins! I heard some men talking on the phone and . . . "

"Whoa, son! Wait a second!" his father interrupted, smiling and throwing up his hands. "Boris told me about the phone call, and there's no kidnapping plot."

Derrick stared at his father in confusion.

"No plot? But Dad, I heard them planning to capture the dolphins!"

His father smiled patiently, as if explaining a difficult math problem.

"Boris said the police told him they had gotten several other reports from people who had overheard strange messages on their cordless. The police said it's probably weather-related. The phones are picking up signals from fishing boat radios, or even television satellites. You probably picked up part of a television cartoon."

A cartoon? The voices he had overheard on the telephone hadn't sounded like part of a cartoon.

"It wasn't a fishing boat or a television show, Dad," he said.

The smile slowly left his father's face, replaced by a tight-lipped look that told Derrick his dad was growing impatient.

"Well, the police say it was," his father said. "But you don't need to worry anyhow. Boris needed to catch up on some maintenance work, so he'll be at the center later than usual tonight."

Suddenly, his father grimaced.

"Oh, no," he moaned wearily. "I just realized I left my briefcase in the office and there are some papers I need to review tonight. Oh, well, too late to worry about it now. I'm starving."

He headed into the kitchen.

"Kerri invited me to dinner at her house," Derrick said. "Is it OK with you?"

"Sure," his dad said. "Just don't stay out too late."

After calling Kerri back, Derrick put on a clean Clueless Hairballs T-shirt and dashed out the door. The sun was setting, and it was cooler now. Far out at sea, a gray curtain of fog slowly spread across the water.

He was impatient to tell Kerri what had happened. Maybe she could help him make sense of it. Perhaps the police and his father were right, he thought. Maybe it was part of a cartoon.

Whatever it was, I'll know after tonight, he thought — not realizing what a long night it would turn out to be.

# Chapter Eight

Fog oozed in from the ocean.

It was a thick, wet fog that seemed to devour any object that came near its ghostly wisps. Pilings, palm trees, stars, the lights of distant ships — all slowly vanished before that vast gray wall.

As Derrick watched the fog creeping across the bay, he had an uncomfortable feeling it was about to swallow him up, too.

He and Kerri were crouched beside the research center. Hiding behind a stack of wooden crates, they could see anyone who entered the center through the front door. They also could keep an eye on the dock in back.

"What time do you think it is?" Derrick whispered.

"Dunno," Kerri whispered back. "I didn't wear a watch."

The bay was eerily silent. The fog seemed to have swallowed up the normal sounds of waves and wind-tossed palms. Derrick shivered.

"Maybe we should leave," he said. "I don't think anyone is coming."

Kerri shook her head.

"Not yet."

This was all her idea. After dinner, when Derrick told her about the phone call he had overheard, she had listened intently. She didn't laugh. She didn't accuse him of making it up. She just listened, her eyes wide and gleaming.

When he had finished, she said something that almost took his breath away.

"We've got to stop them," she said.

"What do you mean?"

"We've got to help the dolphins. We've got to go to the center and make sure they aren't kidnapped."

Derrick suddenly felt queasy, as if he had eaten too much pudding for dessert.

"But maybe Dad is right," he said weakly. "Maybe it was just a problem with the phone."

Kerri shook her head again.

"I don't think so," she said. "Besides, how can it hurt to check things out?"

Derrick had no answer. So when Kerri's mother fell asleep watching television after dinner, they slipped out of the house and ran down the beach to the research center.

When they reached the center, they saw that Boris was working late, just as he had told Derrick's father.

Then, perhaps thirty minutes after they hid themselves behind the pile of boxes, a car had pulled up in front of the door, not ten feet from their hiding place.

It was Derrick's father.

He knocked on the door. When Boris opened it, Derrick saw a flash of his surprise on his face. There was a low murmur of voices, and then his father went inside.

"Why is he here?" Kerri had whispered.

"I don't know," Derrick said. Then he remembered what his dad had said.

"He forgot his briefcase. I'll bet he came back to get it."

That seemed hours ago, and Derrick's father was still inside. From time to time Boris emerged from the rear of the research center and stood on the dock, looking across the darkened bay.

What could Boris and his dad be doing in there, Derrick wondered. His knees were beginning to ache from crouching behind the crates. And he wasn't looking forward to finding his way home in the fog.

"I think we should leave now," he whispered. "My dad will be worried if he gets back home before I do."

"Don't be so impatient," Kerri replied. "Don't you think it's kind of neat? It's like we're spies in a movie."

Derrick let out a long sigh and leaned against the wall.

He did not want to be a spy in a movie. Spies were shot by other spies. He wanted to be safe at home reading a good book. The whole thing was starting to seem dumb to him now, dumb and scary.

Finally, Kerri stood up and stretched.

"I guess you're right," she said. "We might as well leave."

They were just starting to emerge from their hiding place when they heard a faint throbbing sound float towards them out of the ocean fog.

Both of them froze, looking uncertainly at one another.

"What do you think it is?" Kerri asked, her voice quivering.

Derrick listened. The sound grew louder and deeper. It was moving towards them.

"Gotta be a boat," he said. "A big boat. Maybe

it's a tug that got off course."

They ducked back down. As the sound grew louder, Derrick peered around the crates, towards the bay. His heart throbbed in his chest, and his throat felt tight and dry.

At first, he saw nothing except the fog. Then a shape began to emerge from the gauzy grayness.

As it materialized before him, he sucked in his breath sharply.

It was a boat.

A long black boat that seemed to glide above the waves like a giant bat.

A boat that he had seen once before.

And it was heading straight towards them.

# **Chapter Nine**

"That's it!" Derrick whispered. "That's the boat I saw the day I bumped into you at the beach!"

Kerri studied the vessel as it moved across the bay. "I think it's a hydrofoil," she said. "That's why it has two hulls. Hydrofoils are kind of like big pontoon boats, only much faster."

The boat idled forward until it nudged against the dock. A figure sprang down with a coil of rope and tied the boat up.

Derrick tried to make out the man's features, but darkness and fog obscured his face.

Another figure appeared on the ship's upper deck and spoke to the first man. Then both disappeared back into the ship.

Kerri shrank back against the wall. Her lower lip trembled. "What do we do now?" she said.

Why ask me, Derrick thought to himself. He wanted to say something sarcastic to her — like reminding her that coming to the center had been her lame-brained idea.

He remained silent, watching the boat for a few more moments. Then he settled back against the wall beside her. If I were Hercules, or Perseus with a magic sword and shield, I would know what to do, he thought.

But he wasn't an invincible hero. He was just an overweight kid with bad eyesight who had gotten mixed up in a bad mess.

He wanted nothing more than to run away from there as fast as he could. And that's just what he planned to do as soon as he warned his father.

"We've got to tell my dad and Boris," he whispered. "Maybe they can call the shore patrol."

Kerri nodded.

Derrick leaned forward and took another look towards the boat. No one was coming up. He leaned back and took a deep breath.

"Ready?" he whispered.

Kerri nodded again. Derrick slipped past her, moving silently along the wall towards the door. As Kerri followed him, her foot caught the edge of one of the crates and it clattered to the ground.

Derrick froze in his tracks, his heart beating wildly. He listened for sounds from the boat.

But he heard nothing.

Maybe the fog had muted the noise of the crate so that it didn't reach the boat, he thought. After a few moments more, he crept towards the door.

He rapped softly and waited.

"I'm really scared," Kerri whispered. "I think we should leave."

Derrick knocked again.

Finally, they heard a click. A sliver of light appeared as the door slightly opened.

"Who's there?" Boris whispered.

"It's me," Derrick said, standing so that Boris could see him. "You and dad have got to get out. The kidnappers are here. I saw their boat."

The door opened further.

Derrick could see Boris now, standing just inside the doorway. He did not look happy to see them. The light gleamed from his shaved head, and his eyes glowered down at Derrick and Kerri.

Derrick was surprised to see that he was wearing a wet suit. One hand held a partially eaten banana; the other was behind his back.

"Get in here — quick," Boris hissed, seizing Derrick by the shoulder and pulling him inside.

When they were inside, Boris closed and locked the door.

As Derrick looked around, he was surprised to

see that much of the water had been drained from the holding tank. It was now little more than a wading pool, barely covering the dolphins' backs.

"Where's Dad?" he asked. "We've got to get out of here and call the police. The kidnappers are already at the dock."

He heard a muffled groan behind him.

He turned around.

His father lay on the floor. His hands and feet were bound with thick cord. Silver duct tape covered his mouth. His dark hair was matted and sweaty. His frightened eyes darted from Derrick to Boris to Kerri.

Derrick felt as if he had stepped into a horrible dream — a dream even more terrifying than drowning. The floor seemed to tilt beneath his feet. He felt as if he were going to fall down.

He slowly turned back towards Boris. There was a gun in his hand. A cruel smile flickered across his lips.

"It looks like your father got tied up in his work," he said with a smirk.

Then Derrick realized what the gruff-voiced man on the phone had meant about their "man inside."

Boris was working with the kidnappers.

Even amid his fear, Derrick felt a flash of anger towards the man who had betrayed his father.

Voices called from the back of the building. One of the big double doors swung open, and two men strode forward.

One of them was short and thin, with wisps of red hair standing out from the sides of his head. The other was taller and much heavier, and he walked with a slight limp. Both wore wet suits.

"Well, well, what have we here?" the short man said in a deep, gruff voice that Derrick recognized from the conversation he had overheard. "It looks like some unexpected guests have joined our little party."

The tall, stocky man with the limp looked nervously at Boris. "What's going on?" he asked in a thin, whispery voice. "You didn't say nothing about kidnapping any kids. I thought we were just getting dolphins."

Boris lazily waved the gun towards Derrick and Kerri.

"Relax, Rocky," he said. "They're with the dolphin guy. I wasn't expecting them to drop by, but they aren't going to cause any trouble. Who knows — they might even be of use."

The stocky man looked at Boris skeptically.

"Whaddaya mean? How could they be of use?"

Boris shrugged. He took a bite from his banana.

"Who knows?" he said. "You never can tell when you might need a little shark bait."

# Chapter Ten

Derrick's wrists and ankles ached from the rope knotted around them.

He lay on his side in darkness, somewhere inside the boat. Kerri lay beside him. From time to time he heard her soft, frightened sobs.

How long had they had been there? Several hours, at least.

After tying them up, Boris had carried them aboard the boat. Afterward, they heard heavy thumps and scrapes above them. The boat wallowed in the water as it took on more weight.

Derrick knew they were loading the dolphins.

While they were still in the research center, Derrick had seen the tall, heavy man named Rocky setting up a winch that held a large canvas sling. He recognized the sling as the one his father and Boris used to remove dolphins from the pool.

The boat must have a holding pool on the deck, Derrick realized.

From the engine's powerful drone and the boat's rhythmic rocking, Derrick knew they were speeding across water.

He wondered what had happened to his father. The last time he had seen him, he was lying on his side in the research center, his terrified eyes locked onto Derrick's.

"I'm scared," Kerri said in a shaky voice. "They're going to kill us, aren't they?"

She cried for a long time before falling asleep. Even then, she stirred and moaned as if tormented by feverish nightmares.

Derrick did not want to sleep. He was afraid of what he might dream. He was afraid that he might never wake up.

He thought of his mother and of the friends he might never see again back home in North Carolina. He thought of his safe, warm bed back at his father's house in Dolphin Bay.

Maybe I really am in my own bed, dreaming, he thought; when I wake up, it will be another sunny morning at the beach.

And he thought surely he was dreaming when, sometime later in the night, he heard voices murmuring nearby.

It was the kidnappers, discussing their plans.

He couldn't hear everything. But what he heard was enough to summon horrific visions of destruction and death.

The kidnappers planned to make the U.S. government pay them a billion dollars by threatening the country with nuclear disaster.

They had stolen three small nuclear bombs. The dolphins would be their delivery system.

Using his father's research, the kidnappers had built three sonar-sending devices and hidden them in three different places. To show that they could do what they threatened to do, they would send the first dolphin to destroy Miami Beach.

Then, if the government did not deliver the billion dollars, they would destroy a second city, and then a third.

Lying in the darkness, Derrick tried to make sense of what he had heard. No one could be that mad, he thought. No one could be that greedy for money.

He had always thought that sharks and killer whales were the great menaces of the ocean.

But now he realized there were far more dangerous creatures that cruised those waters.

As his eyelids grew heavy, he imagined himself as Perseus, ripping the ropes from his wrists and overpowering the three men.

He was still thinking of that when he slipped into a fretful sleep, dreaming that fire rained from the sky and he was unable to protect himself, even with a magic shield.

\*　　\*　　\*

Derrick was awakened by someone roughly shaking his legs.

It was morning. The boat's engine had stopped. Beyond the doorway, he heard the whisper of waves.

He bolted awake.

Someone was standing above him. Holding a knife.

It was Boris.

"What are you doing?" Kerri asked in a trembling voice.

"Watch and see," Boris smirked.

He raised the knife and slashed at Derrick.

As Kerri screamed, Derrick felt the ropes drop from his ankles. Then, snickering, Boris cut the ropes around his wrists. After freeing Kerri, he motioned towards the door.

"On your feet," he grunted. "Your little holiday cruise is almost over."

Derrick didn't like the sound of that.

They walked down a narrow passageway that led to a short flight of stairs that rose to an open hatch.

Derrick could smell the ocean. Above him was a patch of blue sky.

Then they were on the ship's deck. It was even larger than Derrick had imagined — at least as large as a basketball court. Behind him was the ship's cabin, with its satellite dishes and antennas.

They were surrounded by rolling blue waves. About fifty yards off the stern of the boat was a small island.

At the other end of the deck, Charlie and Rocky were standing in what appeared to be a large wading pool. They watched Derrick and Kerri approach.

As Boris nudged them towards the pool, Derrick saw gray shapes in the water. That's where they had put the dolphins. When they reached the pool, Boris told them to stop.

"I still think it's a bad idea," Boris said to Charlie. "We should have thrown them overboard last night. Always get rid of the evidence."

Charlie scowled at Boris.

"Let me make the plans, OK?" he said. "If we need them later, we'll know where they are. Now get them into the skiff and get them over there."

Glaring at Charlie, Boris pushed Derrick towards the back of the boat. He ordered Derrick and Kerri to get into a small rubber dinghy with an outboard motor. Once they were seated, Boris untied the line and cranked the engine. Then he turned the dinghy around and headed towards the island.

A few minutes later, when they were still several yards off shore, he cut the engine.

"OK, kids," he said. "Welcome to your new home."

Kerri and Derrick looked at him in confusion.

"What do you mean?" Derrick asked. His mouth was dry, but his hands were sweaty.

"I mean get out of the boat. Scram. Vamoose," Boris scowled. "Hit the water."

Derrick started to protest.

"Wait," he said. "What did you do with my father? Where is he?"

Boris laughed.

"Your father is fish food," he said. "He's swimming with the sharks. Just like you're going to be."

Then with a sudden motion of his muscular

arm, he flung Derrick into the water. Kerri tumbled into the water behind him.

"I can't swim," Derrick shrieked. "I'll drown."

Boris laughed again.

"Now you got the right idea, kid," he said.

Then he cranked the engine and roared away.

# Chapter Eleven

As Boris sped away, Derrick knew there would be no dolphin to save him this time. He thrashed about, sputtering and spewing like a wounded seal.

The water was cold. He quickly lost strength as he struggled to stay afloat.

He began sinking.

He was aware of the blue sky above him, the gray sea churning at his chin, and the horrible knowledge that death was near.

Then an arm wrapped around his chest and buoyed him upward.

"Kick!" Kerri shouted. "Don't panic. Just kick and let me guide you."

Derrick tried to calm himself enough to follow her directions. He managed only a weak kick or two before a wave broke over his head. Coughing and sputtering, he clutched at Kerri.

"Stop!" she shouted. "Help me kick! The current's carrying us past the island."

Derrick could feel the underwater flow pushing them out to sea. Kerri gasped for air beside him as she struggled to tow him and keep herself afloat.

She could make it to the island easily if she weren't trying to save me, Derrick thought.

He kicked harder and waved his hands in the water. At first, it made no difference. Then he sensed that they were beginning to make a little headway.

"That's it, Derrick! Keep it up!" Kerri shouted again, redoubling her own efforts.

When it seemed they were both too exhausted to swim one more stroke, they finally drew close enough to the island to wade ashore.

They staggered a few steps up out of the surf and collapsed onto the rocky beach. As he drew great heaving chestfuls of air, Derrick thought it had never felt so wonderful simply to breathe.

"We made it!" Kerri said. "We're here!"

Yes, Derrick thought. But where is *here*?

He surveyed the little outcropping where they now sat.

Derrick estimated the island was about the size of the little park where he often played back home. It took only half an hour or so for him and Kerri to explore the entire surface.

It was mainly black rock, with a few stunted palm trees and tall ferns sprouting from the interior. The shore was covered with more black rocks, a few shells and puddles of gray sand.

"Where do you think we are?" Kerri asked.

They were sitting on a large stone, staring towards the sea.

"I don't know," Derrick answered. "We probably traveled pretty far last night. That's a fast boat."

He picked up a small stone and tossed it into the surf. As it vanished into the water, he thought of his father disappearing into the churning ocean waves. Derrick hadn't even had a chance to say good-bye. And he hadn't had a chance to tell his father how much he loved him.

Kerri put a hand on his shoulder.

"I'm sorry about your dad," she said softly.

Derrick nodded and picked up another rock and threw it farther into the ocean. It glinted for a moment before hitting the waves. It reminded him of Boris's gleaming, bald head, and he felt a flash of anger.

It was all Boris's fault. Without Boris, the kidnap plot wouldn't have worked. Without Boris, they wouldn't be there. Without Boris, Derrick's dad would still be alive.

Then the anger faded, and Derrick felt sad and scared again. Here they were on an island in the middle of nowhere, with no food, no water and no way of escaping.

He turned towards Kerri. "I'm not sure we're any better off here than in the ocean, but thanks for helping me," he said. "I would have drowned if it weren't for you."

Kerri pursed her lips and turned away.

"Why did you lie to me about being able to swim?" she said. "That day I pushed you into the pool, you could have been hurt . . . really hurt."

"I never really lied about it," Derrick said. "I just let you believe something that wasn't true."

"But why?"

Derrick picked up another rock and squeezed it.

"I don't know," he said. "I guess I was afraid if you knew the truth, you wouldn't want to be my friend anymore."

Kerri looked at him in disbelief.

"Just because you couldn't swim? Why would that have anything to do with being friends?"

Derrick clenched the rock harder. Then he flung it far out to sea.

"Pudgy guys with bad eyesight usually aren't very popular," he said. "Heroes are popular. Hercules, the strong guy from Greek mythology, was popular. But not pudgy guys who get trapped by beach chairs."

Kerri slowly shook her head.

"Sharks are great swimmers," she said. "But I wouldn't want one for a friend."

Derrick gave a weak smile. He took a few steps down the shoreline.

He had bent to pick up another rock when he noticed the pinkish curl of a conch shell half-buried in the gray sand.

It's odd to see a shell like that here, he thought. All the other shells are a dingy gray.

He tugged the shell out of the sand.

"Hey," he called to Kerri. "Look what I found."

She was still sitting on the rock and hadn't heard him. He brushed sand off the shell and swished it around in the water. Back in Florida, he thought, this would be worth keeping. But it wouldn't do them any good here.

He cocked his arm, preparing to hurl it out into the ocean.

"What a pretty shell," Kerri said. She had left the rock and was standing beside him. "Did you see if you could hear the ocean in it?"

"I don't need a shell for that," Derrick said.

Seeing Kerri frown, he slowly lifted the shell to his ear. He listened for a moment.

Then his face turned white, and he almost dropped the shell into the water.

"What's wrong?" Kerri said.

Derrick looked at her as if he had just seen a ghost.

"The conch shell spoke to me," he said.

# <u>Chapter Twelve</u>

"It's not talking," Kerri said. "That's how conchs sound. Try it again."

Derrick raised the shell to his ear, a doubtful expression on his face. He really didn't want to hear a seashell speaking. They had enough problems already.

But as he held it to his ear, there was no doubt. What he heard was not the ocean.

"Let me outta here!" a tiny voice called. "Hey, don't shake this thing. You're making me dizzy!"

Derrick lowered the shell.

"I heard it again," he said. "Something is in there."

Kerri's lips tightened in irritation. "This is no time for stupid jokes," she said, whirling around and striding away.

Derrick watched her go, then stared again at the shell.

It seemed impossible that it had spoken to him. But it also seemed impossible that he had been abandoned on an island by dolphin kidnappers. Yet, here he was.

And there the shell was. He raised it to his ear again.

"For Zeus's sake, stop bouncing me around like that," the voice said. "Now get me out of here!"

Derrick hesitated. The only thing dumber than listening to a seashell talk was talking back to one. But — he looked around — Kerri wasn't paying any attention.

"What do you want me do?" he asked the shell.

"Get me out of here!" the voice replied. "Zounds, boy, you're goofier than a Gorgon. Break the shell and free me!"

Derrick held the shell over a flat rock. It's probably not a good idea to break it, he thought. But then, how could things be any worse?

He dropped the shell. It shattered with a loud crack.

Immediately, a white cloud spewed up from the fragments, rising like a column of smoke. When the smoke cleared, Derrick found himself staring at a wild-looking old man with gleaming blue eyes and a shock of white hair that rose like a tidal wave from his broad forehead. He wore a white robe and carried a tri-pronged spear.

"Who are you?" Derrick gasped.

The old man's eyes turned stormy and his lips curved into a scowl.

"I'm Poseidon, ruler of the seas and all that dwell therein," he barked. "Like maybe you were expecting Helen of Troy?"

Derrick stood dumbfounded.

This can't be happening, he thought. Poseidon was just a figure from Greek mythology. He never really existed. He turned to call Kerri, but saw that she was already walking slowly towards him, an expression of disbelief on her face.

So I'm not hallucinating, Derrick thought. Kerri sees him, too.

"Where did you come from?" she said to the old man in a stunned voice barely above a whisper.

He snorted and thumped his spear handle against the ground.

"Jumping jellyfish!" he roared. "You're both as dense as donkeys! I'm Poseidon! I came out of the ocean."

"Actually, you came out of a shell," Derrick said hesitantly. "How did you get trapped in there anyhow?"

Poseidon's face eyes glinted with anger, and

his white hair bristled.

"Hera tricked me again," he muttered. "She wants one of my perfect pearls. Just wait'll I get my hands on her . . . "

Derrick knew from his study of Greek mythology that Hera was Poseidon's sister. It must be some sort of family feud, he thought.

Suddenly Poseidon's eyes swept around the island, as if noticing it for the first time. His eyes came to rest on Derrick and Kerri.

"How did you two get here?" he asked. "Where are your parents?"

"We were kidnapped," Derrick said.

"Yeah, along with Derrick's dad's dolphins," Kerri added.

"And they killed my dad," Derrick said, feeling an ache of sadness.

Poseidon raised his hands. "Hold your chariots," he said. "Now, start from the beginning."

As the old man sat on a rock, Derrick and Kerri told him about the phone call, the night at the research center and their abduction. After they finished, Poseidon shook his head heavily from side to side.

"Sounds like you got tangled up with some real stinky fish," he said. "Somebody needs to put those guys on a fast boat to Hades."

"Will you help us?" Derrick asked hopefully.

Poseidon shook his head.

"I don't like to get involved in the affairs of mortals. It usually just makes things worse," he said. "In fact, I'd better get back into the ocean. No telling what Moby Dick has been up to while I was away."

The old man rose to his feet and began wading into the water. Derrick's shoulders sagged.

"Wait a minute!" he cried. "I freed you from the shell. In a way, I saved your life. Shouldn't you at least grant me a wish or something?"

"If you want a wish, find yourself a stupid genie," the old man barked with a laugh.

As Derrick watched Poseidon's broad back, he felt anger rising in his blood. First Boris had left them there to die. Now they were being abandoned again, and this strange old man found it funny.

Fists clenched at his side, Derrick jumped up and ran after him.

"I'll bet you're not even a real god," he shouted. "You're just a worthless old fake."

The old man slowly turned around.

"Not a real god, eh?" he said.

His fingers tightened on his spear. His eyes squeezed shut. His brow furrowed.

To Derrick's amazement, dark clouds boiled up on the horizon and scudded towards the island. The wind began blowing, softly at first, then harder. Lightning spat from the sky. Thunderclaps shook the ground.

Kerri screamed and ran towards the middle of the island.

The wind howled around Derrick. Rain lashed his face. He was scared out of his wits, but he refused to run. He stood defiantly on the shore, his fists clenched, staring at Poseidon.

Then, when it seemed the wind would snatch him away like a kite, the storm ended. The rain stopped. The clouds cleared. The sun burned from a blue sky.

Poseidon let loose a booming laugh and walked back up onto the shore. His eyes twinkled as he put a huge hand on Derrick's shoulder.

"You need to watch your tongue, lad," he told him. "But I like your spunk. Maybe there is a way I can help you."

# **Chapter Thirteen**

After Poseidon finished speaking, Derrick remained silent for several minutes.

He stared towards the sea, thinking about what it would be like to swim beneath the cold, gray waves, sharing an underwater world with sharks and rays and electric eels and other dangerous creatures.

"Let me get this straight," he said. "You're offering to trade places with me for three days. I become Poseidon, with all your powers, and you become me, with all my weaknesses."

Poseidon nodded.

"That's basically it, with certain restrictions," he said. "You'll be me only while in the water. When you emerge from the water, even if only for a few minutes, you become Derrick again — until you return to the water. And at the end of three days, no matter where you are, or what you're doing, you become Derrick again, permanently."

"And while I'm you, exactly what kind of

powers will I have?"

"You can stir up storms, make volcanoes erupt, hurl thunderbolts, boss big fish around — that sort of thing. Oh, and you can stay underwater a long time without breathing."

Derrick didn't relish the idea of staying underwater for any amount of time. And even with Poseidon's powers, he didn't know whether he could catch the kidnappers. He would be searching for one boat on a big ocean.

But what was the alternative?

If he remained on the island, he and Kerri would starve to death. He would soon be a skeleton wearing a Clueless Hairballs T-shirt.

Not exactly the ideal weight-loss program.

Poseidon's blue eyes bored into him. "Well, lad," he said. "What do you want to do — swim with the sharks, or crawl with the crabs?"

Kerri, who had listened in silence to their discussion, turned to Derrick. "I know it's scary," she said. "But it may be our only chance to survive."

Derrick took a deep breath and slowly exhaled. "OK," he said. "I'll do it. What do we do first?"

Poseidon smiled and extended the trident towards Derrick. "Hold this for a moment," he said.

As Derrick's hand closed around the smooth

wooden handle of the spear, he was surprised by its warmth. Then his hand and arm started to tingle. It felt like an electrical charge was coursing through his body.

Something was happening.

"Just hold on," Poseidon said. "This will only take a minute."

Then, to Derrick's astonishment, it was no longer Poseidon standing in front of him. It was Derrick. He was looking at himself. Which must mean . . .

He looked down. He was much taller than he had been a moment earlier. Instead of a Clueless Hairballs T-shirt, he wore a white robe. He put a hand to his head and was startled to feel a mass of long hair instead of his buzz cut.

Kerri stared at him

"Derrick," she whispered. "Is that really you?"

He nodded.

"It's me."

His voice was loud and deep. It was a very grownup voice. An Olympian voice.

Gripping the spear more tightly, Derrick looked down at Poseidon, who was grinning up at him as if enjoying a great joke.

"Now what do I do?" Derrick asked.

"Hey, don't ask me," Poseidon-turned-Derrick

said with a laugh. "I'm just a kid."

So am I, Derrick thought — I just had a weird growth spurt. He turned and walked down to the edge of the water. Kerri followed a few steps behind.

"Well," Derrick. "I guess it's time to get my feet wet."

With that, he thumped his spear against the ground and, using it like a walking stick, waded into the water.

"Good luck," Kerri called, waving from the beach.

As the cold water rose around his waist, Derrick turned and waved good-bye.

"I'll be back," he said, wondering, even as he spoke, whether he really would.

Then he took a few more steps and vanished beneath the waves.

# Chapter Fourteen

As the water closed over his head, what surprised Derrick most was his calmness.

Moments before, as the waves broke against his chest, he had been afraid — very afraid. It was the same fear he had felt the first time he descended alone into the dark basement of his home. With each halting step, he was leaving the familiar world for something shadowy and unexplored.

But now that he was underwater, it did not feel as if he were entering an alien landscape. It felt as if he were returning home after a long absence.

Surprisingly, he could see quite well underwater. Although cold, the water was clear and bright with sunshine. Schools of small fish darted around him, their scales flashing like bits of glass. The ocean floor was rocky and sloped sharply away from the island.

And it was quiet. As quiet as if his ears had been stuffed with cotton. The only thing he could hear was the muted brush of waves washing up on the island behind him.

He took three more steps. Then he simply lifted his trident, his three-pronged spear, leaned forward — and swam away.

Swimming was much more fun than Derrick had imagined. He glided through the water with lazy kicks of his feet. Then he discovered that he didn't even need to kick.

All he had to do was imagine himself cruising through the water, and it happened. When he imagined speeding up, he sped up. When he imagined slowing down, he slowed down. When he imagined turning in a particular direction, he immediately veered that way.

Awesome, he thought. My mind is controlling my motion.

He imagined himself diving towards the bottom of the ocean. Instantly he found himself plunging down into the depths. The water grew darker and colder.

He began seeing strange fish with small bodies and huge mouths full of teeth like ivory needles. Deeper yet, he saw fish with glowing dots on their sides, like lights on a ship.

Then he saw the sea monster.

It was huge — as long as four cars parked bumper to bumper. At one end of its gray cylindrical body were two fins. At the other end was a writhing knot of long tentacles that reminded Derrick of Medusa's snaky hair.

The thing had two green eyes as big as teacups. And they were staring straight at him.

Derrick changed course, passing within a few feet of the waving tentacles. That's when he realized it wasn't really a monster, just a giant squid. But scary even so.

He shot up towards the surface and broke through the waves. In any direction, all he could see were miles and miles of endless rolling waves.

How am I going to find one boat on this great big ocean, he wondered.

It seemed hopeless, especially in only three days. For a moment, he considered going back to the island and telling Poseidon the deal was off.

But he wasn't even sure he could even find the island again. Besides, he had to try to find the kidnappers and stop their terrible plot.

With a weary sigh, he pointed his spear towards the horizon and cut through the waves.

He swam for hours. During that time, he saw several freighters and ocean liners steaming across the water. He even saw a giant aircraft carrier.

He passed floating jellyfish and giant clumps of

seaweed. But he didn't see anything that remotely resembled the big black boat.

Finally, sometime in the late afternoon, he stopped swimming. He hadn't realized that Greek gods got tired, but he was exhausted.

He floated on his back in the water, staring up into the blue depths of the sky.

It's hopeless, he thought. My first day is almost over, and I'm no closer to finding the boat than I was before. I might as well still be my old helpless self, back on the island with Kerri.

He flipped over onto his stomach. He was slowly paddling through the water, lost in doubt and discouragement, when he saw something that made him gasp with fear.

Not twenty feet away, jutting up from the water, was a shark fin. A *big* shark fin.

As he watched, it began slicing through the water in a slow lazy circle.

He tried to remain calm. The shark was not moving towards him.

Not yet, anyhow.

Maybe it was just curious and would swim away after checking him out. If it did try to attack him, at least he had a weapon — the sharp-tipped trident.

But as he looked at the spear-like weapon in his hand, Derrick realized he probably didn't need to fear the shark at all.

He was Poseidon, ruler of the seas. The shark should obey his bidding.

"Shoo, shark!" he shouted. "Go home, boy! Go home!"

The shark continued to circle him. Then, to his distinct unhappiness, a second fin appeared beside the first.

And then a third fin.

And a fourth.

Soon, he was surrounded by dozens of big fins. And all of them were attached to very big sharks with very sharp teeth.

"Go away! Scram!" he shouted again.

But it was no use. He wondered if Poseidon had lied. Maybe he hadn't given Derrick any special powers after all.

But then, the sharks weren't attacking him, either. They simply stayed at a respectful distance, going around and around him.

It's almost as if they're waiting for a signal, he thought. But what kind of signal? A dinner bell?

Why can't they just swim away and leave me alone, he thought.

The sharks abruptly ceased circling and began swimming away.

Whoa! Derrick thought. How did that happen?

He imagined the sharks turning back around and circling him again.

As if on cue, the sharks swam back and resumed their slow circling.

It's just like when I'm swimming, he thought. All I have to do is imagine what I want them to do, and they do it.

He had a flash of inspiration.

There were dozens of sharks, and they were exceptionally swift swimmers. What if they could help him?

Closing his eyes, he imagined the herd of sharks fanning out to the four corners of the ocean. It would be like having dozens of underwater spies searching for the kidnappers' boat.

He opened his eyes, wondering what he would see.

The sharks were already zipping away, cutting through the water like a squadron of submarines.

But as he watched the sharks speeding away, Derrick worried that they wouldn't be able to find the right boat in time.

# **Chapter Fifteen**

Derrick was surprised at how quickly one of the sharks returned.

He was floating in the water, wondering what Kerri and the real Poseidon were doing back on the island, when a fin sliced towards him.

The shark raised its great toothed snout out of the water and seemed to point in a particular direction.

It wanted him to follow.

He set out after it, swimming as fast as he could. The shark's course went almost directly towards the setting sun. Derrick's eyes swept across the horizon, searching for a familiar shape. Finally, he saw it.

Outlined against the fading light was a small dark shape.

That must be it, he thought, swimming faster.

But as he drew nearer, he saw that the shark had been mistaken.

It was a big, black boat, and it had satellite

dishes on top. But it wasn't the kidnappers' boat.

Derrick sighed and rolled over onto his back. He let the cold waves wash over him. He was so tired.

When the fin appeared beside him again, he ignored it. He was too tired to swim anymore. It would be dark soon.

Then the shark raised its head out of the water. Derrick realized that this was a different shark. And it was carrying something in its teeth.

Derrick looked more closely. And when he saw what the shark had, he knew it had found the kidnappers' boat.

Hanging from its huge mouth was a banana peel.

\*       \*       \*

It was almost dark when the bat-boat came into view. There was no doubt this time about the ship's identity.

As the boat cruised slowly through the water, Derrick saw a man emerge from the cabin door. It was Boris.

As soon as Derrick saw him, he found himself growing angry again. He wanted to stop the kidnappers. Even more than that, he wanted to get even with

Boris.

Now he had his chance.

Closing his eyes, Derrick imagined a great storm sweeping over the ship. He imagined howling wind and driving rain. He imagined lightning lashing down from the sky. He imagined great waves tossing the boat about like a bar of soap.

He imagined Boris disappearing beneath the churning sea.

As Derrick opened his eyes, he saw dark clouds on the horizon. He heard distant claps of thunder. Gusts of wind tousled his long white hair.

Boris turned from the railing and stared towards the approaching storm. He tried to retreat into the ship's cabin. It was too late. Before he could take two steps, the storm struck.

Waves battered the boat. It rocked and shuddered as if a giant hand were shaking it. At times, the boat seemed to vanish behind sheets of torrential rain. Then it would reappear in a flash of lightning.

Through it all, Boris somehow clung to the railing. But Derrick saw with satisfaction that his face had a look of absolute terror as he tried to keep from being washed overboard.

The boat can't last much longer, Derrick thought. Nothing could survive this storm.

He wondered where the other two kidnappers were hiding. They're probably in the cabin, trying to keep the boat from capsizing, he thought.

Moving closer to the ship, Derrick was able to see through the cabin window. Just as he had thought, Charlie and Rocky were struggling with the boat's controls.

Then, as the boat took a sudden sickening lurch and almost overturned, Derrick realized there was a third man in the cabin with Rocky and Charlie. Derrick could not see his face, but there was something familiar about him.

As Derrick moved in for a closer look, the boat took another lurch. Derrick caught a glimpse of the man's face as he lurched against the window.

It can't be, he thought.

But it was.

Boris had lied to him about his father.

His father hadn't drowned. He was inside the boat.

Derrick was filled with elation and joy. His father was alive!

But his joy quickly vanished as a huge wave bore the boat upward and then slammed it down. Unless Derrick could stop the storm, his father wouldn't be alive much longer.

Quickly, he imagined the storm clouds evaporating. He imagined the rain ending and the seas growing calm.

As quickly as it had begun, the storm ended. The clouds raced away towards the horizon. The thunder died away. The sea settled down to a glassy calmness.

Boris slowly relaxed his grip on the railing. He sank to his knees, looking around him in disbelief. Rocky and Charlie and Derrick's father slowly emerged from the cabin and stood staring at the vanishing clouds.

Derrick couldn't help but smile, thinking about the scene he had just created.

He was still smiling when a white hand erupted from the water beside him and seized his arm. A moment later, a woman's head appeared.

Beside him emerged a woman with eyes as green as emeralds and long red hair that flowed over her shoulders like a mane of flames.

"So there you are!" she cried. "Where have you been? I tell you to take out the trash, and you disappear for a thousand years! I'll bet you were playing poker with Prometheus and your other worthless pals. Well, you're not sneaking away this time."

Before Derrick could pull away, she seized him by the robe and jerked him underwater. He found himself being towed towards the bottom of the ocean as if he were a lizard on a leash.

# **<u>Chapter Sixteen</u>**

As the red-haired woman dragged him into an underwater cave, Derrick realized who she was.

She was Amphitrite, the sea-nymph who was Poseidon's wife. Which meant that she was now his wife.

Poseidon hadn't mentioned this part of the deal, Derrick thought.

Once they got past two manta rays that guarded the cave's entrance, Derrick was astonished at what he saw.

The cave was as spacious as a ballroom. Beautiful shells covered the walls. There was a huge couch and matching chairs made of pink coral, and a table made from a giant turtle shell. This was where Poseidon — the *real* Poseidon — lived.

Amphitrite shoved him onto the couch. She stood above him, staring down angrily with her hands on her hips.

"I simply can't have you running off like that

anymore," she said. "The neighbors start gossiping and the chores pile up."

"But it wasn't my fault," Derrick said. "I'm not really . . . "

"No more excuses," Amphitrite snarled. "You're my husband and I expect you to be here when I need you. Now, here's a list of chores you need to do tomorrow."

She waved a piece of paper.

"First, we're going to the Olympian Mall to get new wallpaper for the bathroom. Then you need to clean out the stables and fix the leaky faucet in the kitchen."

Derrick gave an inward groan. He needed to get back to the kidnappers' boat. It was already night-time — the end of his first day as Poseidon. He couldn't afford to waste time hanging around in a cave.

Suddenly Amphitrite's expression softened. She sat down beside him. Very close beside him.

"You look tired," she said. She put an arm around him and rubbed his shoulders. "You should let me give you a massage."

Derrick edged away.

"Uh — maybe tomorrow night," he stammered. "I'm really tired. I need to get some sleep."

Amphitrite sprang up and flounced away.

"As you please," she snapped. "Just make sure you're still here in the morning."

She held out a small blue bottle.

"Here's a new potion to help you sleep," she said. "Morpheus mixed it for you before you disappeared. He said to take one drop when you have insomnia."

Derrick took the bottle. He faked a yawn.

"Thanks," he said. "I don't think I'll need it tonight."

"Your room is ready," Amphitrite said, gesturing towards a passageway at the end of the room. "Remember, we have a busy day ahead."

After she left, Derrick remained on the couch, absent-mindedly toying with the blue bottle. He would have to wait until Amphitrite was asleep before trying to slip away.

Meanwhile, he might as well look around. He entered the passageway that Amphitrite had indicated.

After going down a narrow tunnel, he found himself in another large cavern. It contained a bed made of whale bone and covered in swan feathers. Then he saw another tunnel leading from this room, and he followed it.

After several twists and turns, he entered another room and stopped, gaping in amazement. Around the room were huge chests overflowing with pearls and gemstones. They spilled out of the boxes and lay scattered about like a child's toys.

Derrick picked up a pearl the size of an egg. Mesmerized by its brilliance, he turned it over in his hand. This would be worth a fortune, he thought.

He picked up an emerald that was almost as large. There were so many beautiful stones, he thought. Certainly, no one would notice if one of them disappeared.

Besides, since this was his house, they rightfully belonged to him. Or at least to Poseidon.

He tucked the pearl into his robe.

He continued down another tunnel. Fascinated by this strange place, Derrick wandered through passageways like a worm working its way through the ground. Stopping for a moment here, backtracking there, he lost all sense of time.

Only when he started trying to make his way back to the main cavern did he realize that he was lost.

He tried several passages, but nothing looked familiar. He wandered from tunnel to tunnel, lost and frightened.

No one will ever find me here, he thought. I'll turn back into my real self, and then I'll die.

Wait — what was that noise? It sounded like the faint whinny of a horse.

Derrick waited. There it was again, and it *was* a horse. It came from a tunnel that branched off to his right.

As Derrick went down this passageway, he heard the sound again — louder this time. Then, moments later, he heard another loud whinny and the unmistakable sound of horses blowing and snorting. And he seemed to detect the smell of fresh manure.

Suddenly the passageway opened into a giant cave-stable.

Derrick rubbed his eyes.

In front of him stood a golden chariot hitched to a team of six huge sea horses. As they saw Derrick, their eyes rolled and flames shot from their mouths.

Now that's my kind of hot wheels, Derrick said to himself.

Hoisting himself into the chariot, he picked up the reins.

"Giddyup!" he shouted.

Nothing happened.

Then he imagined the sea horses swimming with all their might, swiftly pulling the chariot up from the ocean's depths. Immediately, the chariot leaped forward, almost knocking him to the floor.

Fire shot from the sea horses' nostrils as they rocketed through the tunnels. In its mad flight, the chariot banged against the cave walls, sparks shooting up behind it.

They emerged from the cave and the chariot climbed sharply through the water. A few minutes more and it burst through the sea's surface.

The sea horses sat panting in the water, the chariot hissing and smoking as it cooled behind them.

Derrick looked around. It was night. The sky was a dome of darkness, studded with a million stars.

But where was the kidnappers' boat?

At first, he saw nothing except the shimmering tops of waves. Then, at a distance, he saw moving lights. The lights of a boat.

The chariot moved forward again.

Gradually, the lights grew brighter. The shape of the kidnappers' boat emerged from the night.

Derrick let the sea horses pull him as close as he dared without risking detection. Then he gave them a mental command to return to their stable.

The chariot sank away beneath him, and he was alone in the cold water. No one was visible on the deck of the boat, but he could hear the thrumming of its engines. Someone was manning the controls, piloting the boat.

As he drew nearer, he glimpsed the lighted cabin and saw the big man called Rocky at the wheel. The others must be asleep, he thought.

He had to get aboard and find his father.

He swam all around the boat, looking for a way to climb aboard. But the deck was too high above the water. I need a boost from someone with long arms, Derrick thought.

A moment later, he felt himself gripped gently under the arms. Two giant octopus tentacles lifted him out of the water as if he weighed no more than a match stick. The octopus set him down at the rear of the boat and the tentacles slithered away.

Derrick knelt behind a big barrel. As he bent over, he heard something drop onto the deck and roll away.

The sleeping potion had fallen from his toga. He picked it up, relieved to find it intact.

But as he held the bottle, something very strange happened. His hand suddenly shrank. Then he realized that it wasn't just his hand; all of him had shrunk. He was his chubby self again, wearing a Clueless Hairballs T-shirt and ragged cutoffs.

He remembered what Poseidon had said: Every time he came out of the water, he would revert to his true identity.

That won't make this any easier, he thought. He shoved the sleeping potion into his pocket and peered around the edge of the barrel. He could see Rocky in the upper cabin, steering the boat, with his back to Derrick.

*Now.*

Derrick darted from behind the barrel, across the deck, past the dolphin pool and down the hatch leading below deck. Once out of sight, he stopped and took several ragged breaths. His heart was pounding and his brow was sweaty.

He squinted down the narrow passageway. It was dark except for a sliver of light showing under one of the doors.

That must be where dad is, Derrick thought.

He inched towards the door. He listened for sounds behind it. He heard nothing.

He reached for the handle. He had almost touched it when, to his horror, the door suddenly opened.

Derrick shrank back, flattening himself against the wall.

Boris emerged from the room. He was carrying a gun.

Boris stood for a moment in the light, as if listening. Then he walked down the corridor, away from

Derrick, and vanished into another compartment.

Derrick looked through the open door. His father lay on his side on the floor, facing the doorway. His hands and feet were tied with rope.

"Derrick!" he whispered hoarsely. "I thought you were dead! How did you get here?"

Derrick put a finger to his lips. "I'll explain later," he whispered. "Boris is just down the hall. We don't have much time."

What to do? He looked around the room. There was a table. A chair. A half-eaten banana. A magazine.

Wait. A half-eaten banana . . . ?

Derrick pulled the sleeping potion from his pocket. He dribbled a few drops onto the banana. He father watched in puzzlement.

"What are you doing?" he asked. "Derrick, stop playing around. Untie me. Maybe we can overpower Boris when he comes back."

But Derrick was already leaving the room. "I'll be back," he promised. "Just wait."

He saw an expression of alarm on his father's face, as if he feared that Derrick wouldn't return.

Then something cold and hard pressed against the back of Derrick's neck and he heard a familiar snicker.

Boris's bald head gleamed above him. He waved the gun in Derrick's face.

"You're not going anywhere," Boris hissed. "I don't know how you got here, but you won't leave this boat alive again."

# Chapter Seventeen

"How did you get back here?" Boris hissed. "Who helped you?"

Derrick was sitting on the floor beside his father. His hands were tied behind him, but Boris had not bound his ankles. Not yet, anyhow.

Boris sat on the table across from him, pointing the gun between Derrick and his father. Derrick looked at the weapon, then at the banana lying a few inches from Boris's elbow.

When Derrick didn't answer, Boris stood up and walked over to him. He squatted in front of him and stuck the gun in his face.

"I'm not hearing anything," Boris said. "It's much too quiet in here."

Derrick swallowed hard. What could he say — that a weird old man from Greek mythology had gotten released from a sea shell and traded places with him?

He might as well tell Boris that he had hailed a

taxicab or hitched a ride on a hurricane.

Derrick looked again at the banana. Then he had an idea ....

"I'm really hungry," he whined. "Could I have the rest of your banana?"

His father looked at him in shock. He knew that Derrick had put something on the piece of fruit.

Boris seemed momentarily confused.

"Banana? Hungry?" His bald head bobbed in the light. Then a malicious smile split his face.

"Sure," he said, going over to the table. "Sure, have some banana."

He picked up the banana, walked over and squatted beside Derrick. Then, with his face inches from Derrick's, Boris lifted the banana and stuffed the rest of it into his own mouth.

"Ummmmm," Boris said, chewing with exaggerated slowness. "Good banana."

Smiling broadly, he dropped the peel into Derrick's lap.

"You have the rest," he said.

He rose to his feet and turned back towards the desk.

But after a couple of steps, he swayed on his feet. The gun clattered to the floor. Boris's body followed it, thumping down like a sack of sand.

Before Boris hit the floor, Derrick was on his feet. He kicked the gun away from the motionless body.

"Looks like you need a nap," he said. "We've got to get out of here now. There isn't much time. They're going to use the dolphins to blow up some cities."

His father looked up at him with a sad, tired expression.

"I know about the plot," he said. "They forced me to help them. And it's too late to stop it."

"Why is it too late?"

"The sonar signals are already in place. They strapped a bomb to Flash and dumped him into the water. He'll be at Miami Beach in a few hours."

# Chapter Eighteen

Derrick had a momentary vision of Flash swimming through the water harnessed to a bomb.

He imagined a sunny day at the beach, children laughing and swimming and making sand castles. Drawn by the sonar signal, Flash headed straight towards them. Then a gigantic fireball erupted, and Derrick stopped imagining.

"There's got to be something we can do," he said. "Couldn't we jam the signals or something?"

His father shook his head. "You'd have to have a special transmitter to do that. Even then, I'm not sure you could do it."

Derrick struggled to his feet. If he could find something in the room to cut the ropes around his wrists, he could at least free the two of them. That would give them a chance to take over the boat.

"What are you doing?" his father asked.

"Looking for a knife or something else with a sharp edge."

He looked all around the small compartment but saw nothing that might help free them. He would have to look elsewhere.

Derrick headed towards the door.

"Where are you going?" his father asked anxiously. "Don't leave. They're liable to see you."

Derrick hesitated. He would rather remain with his father, but he knew they had no chance of escaping if he did.

"I'll be back," he said. "I just want to look around."

He tiptoed back down the passageway and poked his head up through the hatch.

The eastern horizon was tinged with the pink and purple streaks of approaching dawn. Soon it would be light. A breeze had kicked up, and the boat gently rolled on rising swells.

Derrick climbed the short ladder to the deck and looked around.

Rocky was still in the cabin. Derrick quickly scanned the ship's deck, searching for anything that might serve as a knife. He saw coils of rope, a couple of wooden boxes, a gaff hook on a wooden pole.

But no knife.

Maybe there's something in the stern of the boat, Derrick thought. He peered towards the cabin again. Rocky still seemed to be occupied with the boat's controls.

Crouching as low as he could, Derrick worked his way towards the back of the boat, keeping to the shadows and periodically glancing back at Rocky.

He had almost made it to the rear of the boat when his foot slipped on a wet spot on the deck.

With his hands tied, he couldn't regain his balance. He fell with a crash, knocking over a wooden box that had been leaning against the dolphin pool. Pain shot through his ankle.

In the cabin, Rocky whirled around. He listened and looked into the darkness. Then he turned from the wheel and emerged from the cabin.

Pulling a silver-barreled pistol from the waistband of his pants, he walked towards the back of the boat.

Derrick lay motionless in the darkness, watching.

If he could make it to the side of the boat and jump over, he might be able to escape. But his ankle throbbed with pain. He doubted that he could walk on it, much less sprint across the deck.

He leaned his head against the edge of the dolphin pool and closed his eyes. He felt sick with fear and pain.

He thought of Belle and Dorie floating inches away from him in the shallow pool. And while he was thinking of them, he suddenly opened his eyes.

Steeling himself against the pain of movement and using his last ounce of strength, he heaved himself over the edge of the pool and rolled with a splash into the water beside the two dolphins.

"Hey!" Rocky shouted. "Who's out there?"

Derrick lay on his back in the water, letting it cover him completely. He looked up at the inky sky and the bright stars. He heard Rocky call out again, much closer this time. Then Rocky was standing beside the dolphin pool, looking down at Derrick.

Only, he was no longer Derrick.

Once the water covered him, he became Poseidon again. The rope was gone from his wrists, the pain gone from his ankle.

He waited until Rocky's face was directly over his, squinting down into the pool as if he were looking at a corpse in a casket.

Then, as Rocky leaned closer, Derrick thrust himself up out of the water into the kidnapper's horrified face.

Rocky shrieked and staggered back. As he tried to turn and aim his gun at Derrick, his foot caught on one of the crates and he smashed into the deck.

By then, Derrick had clambered from the pool onto the gunwale of the boat. With one last look at the terrified man lying on the deck, he leaped overboard, plunged into the water and was gone.

# **Chapter Nineteen**

Derrick did not want to leave his father behind on the boat. But time was running out.

He had to find Flash before the bomb exploded.

Back in the ocean as Poseidon, Derrick tried to think of the quickest way to search. There were thousands of dolphins in the sea. He could summon them all; Flash would have to be among them.

But he had no idea how long it might take Flash to swim back to him; the bomb might explode before he arrived.

Perhaps he should swim towards Florida, and hope to overtake Flash somewhere along the way.

But Derrick had no idea where he was, or what direction he should take.

He swam aimlessly through the water. The sun climbed higher above the horizon. It's my second day as Poseidon, Derrick thought, and I'm no closer to solving this mess than I was yesterday.

I can't find a dolphin carrying a bomb. I can't even find Florida.

In any direction, he found the same unchanging scene: Choppy gray water and blue sky. And one other thing: A large coconut floating a few yards in front of him.

Curious, he swam over and reached out to grasp it. Just as his hand touched the coconut, an iron manacle snapped shut around his wrist, and the coconut suddenly was transformed into a big wooden barrel to which he found himself chained.

Then Derrick heard laughter above him.

Looking up, he saw a woman sitting on top of the barrel. At first, he thought it was Amphitrite come to drag him home again. But this woman's hair was curly and black, not red, and she had a long, hooked nose that reminded him of a rusty scythe.

"So," she taunted him. "You didn't like the comfort of my little seashell jail. But I seem to have you over a barrel again."

Hera!

She had trapped Poseidon in the shell, and now she had trapped Derrick. He tugged mightily against the iron manacle, but it was no use. He couldn't break free.

"What do you want?" he sputtered. "I have to

get free . . . There isn't much time . . . "

Hera cackled again and slyly eyed him.

"Of course there's time," she said. "There's an eternity. And you know what I want, so why don't you just hand it over? Something you just found a few moments ago."

As she said this, Derrick remembered the pearl stashed inside his robe. All he had to do was hand it over and she would free him.

But that's not what he did.

"I don't have the pearl," he said.

Hera scowled at him.

"What do you mean? Where is it?"

"I knew you would try to trick me again, so I hid it in the ocean."

"Where in the ocean?"

Derrick took a deep breath. He hoped this worked.

"It's in a big container strapped to a dolphin swimming somewhere in the ocean," he said. "All you have to do now is find it."

Hera eyed him suspiciously.

"How do I find the dolphin?" she asked.

Derrick turned away and shrugged.

"That's your problem," he said, feigning indifference. "But there aren't many dolphins in the ocean with metal cans strapped to them."

Hera studied him for a long time, as if trying to divine his intention. She isn't buying it, Derrick thought.

At that moment, Hera closed her eyes and seemed to tense her upper body. Then she was gone, and in her place a giant eagle sat atop the barrel.

"You better not be lying," the eagle croaked, its golden eyes glaring down at Derrick. "If you are, I'll come back and eat your liver."

With that, the bird spread its huge wings and soared high above the ocean, its head turning to and fro as its powerful eyes peered down into the sea.

Derrick tried to follow it, but pulling the barrel was like trying to tow a barge. He could make little headway, and the eagle soon dwindled to a dot and disappeared.

Frustrated, Derrick gave a sharp tug on the chain. He poked at the barrel with his trident. Then he gave an angry cry and rolled over onto his back.

It's out of my hands now, he thought. There's nothing I can do except wait.

Then he realized that there was one other thing he could do.

Closing his eyes, he imagined a herd of whales circling the kidnappers' boat, corralling it like a lost sheep. At least that would keep it from going any-where for a while, he thought.

Lulled by the waves and the warm sun, he dozed off.

Sometime later, he awoke to a loud boom. Fearing the worst, he looked towards the direction where the sound originated, expecting to see a giant mushroom cloud.

Instead, he saw only a towering bank of clouds in the distance. He relaxed: It was only thunder.

The sun climbed higher in the sky. Half the day is gone, he thought. Hera isn't back. Even disguised as an eagle, she couldn't sort Flash from all the creatures of the sea.

Derrick sighed. He might as well admit it: He had failed. Even with Olympian powers, he was still a klutz.

In a way, he thought, it's even worse to fail when you have great powers, because then there's really no excuse. He felt like crying.

But when he rubbed his eyes a moment later, it wasn't because of tears. He thought he saw something at a distance in the sky. A dot. A black dot, rapidly growing larger.

The dot became a bird, a large bird flying low over the ocean, its wings almost brushing the waves.

A large bird carrying what appeared to be a big fish in its talons.

It was the giant eagle, and it was carrying a dolphin with a metal contraption harnessed to its back. Derrick felt a momentary surge of happiness and hope. The bomb had not gone off yet.

Then his happiness turned to terror as he saw the eagle's eyes burning towards him. This was one angry bird.

"You lied," the eagle croaked. "And now you'll die."

Its talons loosened their hold, and Flash splashed into the ocean. Then with an ear-splitting shriek, the eagle launched itself at Derrick, its beak pointed towards him like the tip of a machete.

His hand fumbled frantically through the folds of his robe. Finally, he clutched the pearl in his hand.

"Catch!" he shouted, and flung his arm towards the sky.

To his horror, the pearl slipped from his grasp and plunged towards the water.

"No!" he screamed.

He lunged against the chain, but the pearl bounced from his fingertips and plopped into the sea. As it vanished from view, the eagle gave another piercing cry and its great curved claws came slashing towards his head.

# **Chapter Twenty**

As the eagle loomed over him, Derrick ducked under the water.

He heard another piercing cry and the bird's talons tore through his long hair, barely missing his scalp. If he had been a split-second slower, Hera would have had his head for lunch.

Derrick hovered a few feet under the surface, unable to dive deeper because of the chain. There was no escape now. Eventually, he would have to surface, and when he did, the eagle would be waiting.

He stared down into the depths where the pearl had vanished.

It's probably on the bottom of the ocean by now, he thought. Or in the belly of a barracuda.

He turned away in despair, resigned to rising to the surface and surrendering to Hera. But a movement deep in the water caught his eye.

Something came towards him.

It was Flash. The bomb was on his back.

And the pearl was in his mouth.

This time, as he grasped the pearl, Derrick made sure he had a good grip. He looked up through the water towards the sky. He couldn't see the eagle, but he knew it was there, its huge golden eyes watching the surface for any sign of movement.

I won't have another chance, he thought.

Propelling himself upward with a mighty kick, he burst through the waves and hurled the pearl into the air. The eagle, which had already started its deadly descent towards him, faltered for a moment in midair. It veered away, swooped up like a rocket and snatched the pearl in its beak.

As the eagle flew away, the manacle fell from Derrick's wrist.

He was free, and Hera was gone.

But there was no time for celebration.

Grasping Flash's harness, he tried to undo the straps. He fumbled with it for a few moments. Then, with a cry of frustration, he ripped them away. He grabbed the bomb and swam towards the ocean floor.

Get out of here *now*, Flash! he thought. Swim as fast and as far as you can.

But he saw with dismay that the dolphin was following him deeper and deeper towards the bottom of the sea.

When he reached the ocean floor, Derrick headed for a craggy underwater trench. He followed it until he came to a cave. He swam inside and he hurled the bomb deep into the passageway. Then he raced for the exit.

Just as he emerged from the cave's mouth, there was a muted explosion deep within the earth. A shock wave rocked the water around him.

That was close, he thought as he swam away.

As he shot up towards the surface, he searched the murky water and prayed for Flash to reappear.

But he could find no trace of the big dolphin that had saved his life again.

# Chapter Twenty-One

Late that evening, after swimming for several hours, Derrick heard a strange humming sound in the water.

It was soulful and sad, as if someone were crying underwater. Then he saw a line of blue humps rising out of the water in the distance, and he realized he was hearing the song of the whales.

It had taken longer to find them than he had expected. He had begun to wonder if they had heeded his command.

But now, they were there in front of him: dozens of humpbacked whales, swimming in a circle and singing their haunting song.

And in the middle of the circle was the big black boat.

Its engines were silent.

Boris, Charlie and Rocky stood at the railing. They stared out at the whales as if trying to determine whether the massive wall of mammals was real or a mirage. Derrick swam underwater and came up at the edge of the boat, hidden from the men but able to hear them.

"Maybe I should shoot one," Boris said. "It might scare them away."

"Don't be an idiot," Charlie's gruff voice replied. "They'd probably attack us and bash the boat to bits."

Rocky limped back and forth in front of the railing.

"Why would they be doing this?" he said. "It's like someone is sending them signals."

Boris turned towards him.

"Maybe someone is," he said, and he walked across the deck and disappeared down the hatch.

A few minutes later he reappeared, marching Derrick's dad in front of him at gun-point. He had untied Mr. Granger's feet but not his hands. Boris nudged him towards the railing.

"So is this *your* little trick?" he asked, poking the gun into Mr. Granger's back.

Derrick's father stared at the ring of whales.

"Astonishing," he said. "This is unique behavior for Cetaceans. There's nothing in any of the research to suggest . . . "

"Cut the bull," Boris hissed. "I know you're

behind this. You're the only one around here who can talk to fish."

Not quite, Derrick thought as he moved away from the edge of the boat just enough to see the men above him.

Boris's face contorted with anger. He pushed the gun deeper between Mr. Granger's shoulder blades.

"You've got ten seconds to tell those whales to scram," Boris said.

Charlie looked at Boris in alarm.

"Calm down," Charlie said. "We're going to need him to send the second bomb."

"There won't *be* a second bomb unless we get out of this," Boris snarled. "And he's the only one who knows how to do that."

He turned back to Derrick's father.

"I'm going to count to three, and if those whales don't start to bale out of here, you're history. One . . . two . . . "

Boris stopped counting.

He stared at the whales, his jaw hanging open, as the great creatures left the circle and swam away, just as Derrick had told them to do.

"Holy catfish!" Charlie marveled. "He really *can* talk to fish!"

He turned to Derrick's dad.

"How did you do that?"

Mr. Granger was too bewildered to speak. He shook his head, shrugged, and watched the whales swim away as if they were an alien life form he had never seen before.

"Come on, come on," Boris barked. "We don't have time to sightsee. Let's get that second bomb in the water before something else happens."

He pushed Mr. Granger over to the dolphin pool. Charlie and Rocky had already attached the canvas sling to the winch and were lowering it into the pool with Dorie and Belle.

Then the two men opened a box and lifted out a harness and a metal canister just like the one Derrick had removed from Flash.

What do I do now? Derrick wondered.

He could destroy the ship with a storm, or split it apart with lightning bolts. But his father might be injured — or worse. Before he could attack the kidnappers, he had to get his father away from them somehow.

The dolphin was ready.

As Derrick watched, Boris tightened the harness and the men lowered the dolphin into the water. It made a couple of slow circles at the end of the boat and then swam away with its deadly burden.

"When will it reach the target?" Rocky asked.

"Early tomorrow morning," Boris said, peeling a banana. "Just in time for breakfast. And when they know we mean business, we'll have a billion dollars for dessert."

As Charlie watched the dolphin through a pair of binoculars, Boris pushed Mr. Granger towards the ladder that led to the pilot house. There they would monitor the dolphin's progress on sonar.

Derrick, however, intended to keep a much closer eye on it.

Quickly catching up with the dolphin, he called it to deeper water. As Belle waited beside him, he removed the bomb from the harness. He dove towards the ocean floor and found another cave where he buried the bomb.

Then, he dove down again. His eyes scanned the murky waters until he found what he was seeking: A sunken battleship.

Searching among its silt-filled holds, he found a large shell that resembled the nuclear bomb he had removed from the harness. He slipped this shell into the harness on Belle's back.

Another search of the sunken ship yielded a length of steel cable.

This had better work, Derrick thought as he and Belle swam towards the surface. He was running out of ideas — and time.

# Chapter Twenty-Two

The next morning Boris, Rocky and Charlie stood at the railing, gazing anxiously out to sea.

"Why would the dolphin disappear from radar?" Rocky asked. "The first dolphin goes off course, and now this one vanishes. Something's not right."

Boris hurled a banana peel into the water.

"We've been sabotaged," he said. "And I know who did it. But he won't do it again."

Boris pulled the gun from his trousers and went below deck. He brought Mr. Granger up to the deck, twisting his arm so forcefully that he cried out in pain.

"Tell us what you did to the dolphin!" Boris shouted, holding the gun to his head. "Tell us or I'll kill you!"

When Mr. Granger made no reply, Boris twisted his arm harder.

"I'm going to count to three," he said.

"One . . . two . . ."

At that moment, Belle surfaced beside the boat and gave a chattering squeal.

"Look — there it is!" Charlie shouted. "And it still has the bomb!"

The men froze. Then a flurry of motion erupted.

"Shoot it!" Rocky yelled. "Shoot before it gets away."

He and Boris fired several shots towards Belle. The dolphin vanished. The men stared into the water.

"I think we got her," Boris said.

Moments later, there was a chattering cry behind them as Belle surfaced on the other side of the boat. The men ran across the deck and fired into the water again.

Belle surfaced behind the boat, then in front of it as the men fired wildly, trying to guess where she would appear next.

"It's no use," Boris shouted. "We can't hit her. We've got to get out of here! That bomb could explode any moment!"

Charlie leaped up the ladder to the control room and hit the switch to start the engines. The motors coughed to life, then died with a loud grinding noise.

Derrick, who had been controlling Belle's

movements, smiled as he watched.

"What happened to the engines?" Charlie shouted.

"Something's wrapped around the propellers," Boris said. "It's some kind of cable."

The dolphin came up a few feet away, gave another skittering cry and vanished again.

"We've got to get out of here," Boris said. "We'll have to use the dinghy."

Cursing one another and the dolphin, the men worked feverishly to lower the rubber raft into the water. Boris positioned a rope ladder over the side and scrambled down. As Charlie and Rocky tumbled into the boat, Boris started the engine.

"What about Granger?" Charlie shouted.

"Let him blow up with his precious dolphin," Boris yelled.

Telling Belle to remain with the big boat, Derrick swam after the dinghy. He caught up with it a mile or so away. As he thrust his white-haired head out of the water and brandished the trident, the men drew back in alarm.

"Stop the boat!" Derrick bellowed. "Surrender and you won't be harmed!"

Boris fired several shots into the water. Derrick dove away and resurfaced at a safer distance.

"This is your last chance!" he shouted. "Surrender now!"

The men fired at him again. As the bullets whizzed past his head like hornets, Derrick felt a surge of anger welling up inside him like a tidal wave. With a thunderous shout, he began swimming in circles around the dinghy.

Faster and faster he circled, until a whirlpool formed around the little boat. Boris tried to steer out of the swirling water, but the vortex was too strong.

With a great sucking noise, the whirlpool began pulling the skiff down.

The men screamed in terror and huddled in the bottom of the boat. As they cowered in fear, Derrick's anger began to subside. Although they had been ready to kill him, he could not do the same to them.

They were utterly evil; but he was no executioner.

Derrick reversed course and began swimming in the opposite direction. But as he swam against the current he had created, trying to slow it, something was terribly wrong. A great weariness fell over him.

He could hardly lift his arms or kick his legs. It was as if he were trying to swim through glue.

Maybe it's this baggy T-shirt that's weighing me down, he thought.

That's when he realized he wasn't Poseidon anymore.

Time had run out.

He was back in his chubby old body. The one that didn't know how to swim. He no longer controlled the seas. He couldn't even control himself.

He heard a scream and looked up to see Boris's bald head, gleaming at the center of the foamy maelstrom. There was another scream and Boris disappeared.

Derrick gave another feeble stroke or two with his arms, trying to escape the roaring funnel of water. It was no use.

Even if he could swim, he could never escape the whirlpool. He was as helpless as a rat in a raging river.

In sending the kidnappers to their fate, he had sealed his own.

## Chapter Twenty-Three

"What happened then?" Kerri asked.

She and Derrick were walking on the beach at Dolphin Bay. It was the last day of Derrick's vacation. Tomorrow, he would fly home to North Carolina.

"I'm not sure," he said hesitantly. "Everything started whirling around, and I felt myself getting dizzy and going underwater. Then it was like a giant wave suddenly rolled up under me, carrying me away from the whirlpool. It was almost like I body-surfed back to the boat and dad pulled me out."

Kerri shook her head.

"That's really wild," she said. "How could a wave come out of a whirlpool?"

"I don't know," Derrick said. "I don't know how any of it could have happened — the kidnapping, Poseidon, the whirlpool . . . "

The beach was almost deserted except for the two of them. A brown dog frolicked in the surf, plunging into the waves and then racing back up the beach. Down the shore, an old man in a faded Hawaiian shirt collected shells, leaning on a walking stick.

"And the Coast Guard didn't find any trace of the three men?"

Derrick turned away so that Kerri couldn't see his face.

"Nothing," he said softly. "Just the rubber dinghy floating upside down."

"It wasn't your fault," Kerri said quickly. "They deserved what they got. You gave them a chance to surrender."

Derrick nodded, but his expression told Kerri it was time to change the subject.

"I'm just glad your father was able to find the coordinates of the island in the ship's computer," she said. "Otherwise, I'd still be out there."

Derrick picked up a shell and studied it. He handed it to Kerri.

"What kind is it?" he asked.

"It's a whelk," she said. "Very pretty."

They were startled by a loud voice behind them.

"Look at this one! Ain't she a beauty?"

It was the old man who had been collecting shells. He held out a big conch.

"You can hear the ocean in there," he said.

"Go ahead — try it."

Underneath a faded Miami Dolphins hat, the old man's hair was long and white. His blue eyes had the icy brightness of a frozen lake.

"Go on!" he said, handing the shell to Derrick. "Give it a listen!"

Reluctantly, Derrick raised the shell to his ear. After a moment, his eyes opened wide with bewilderment. He stared up at the old man, unable to speak.

The man reached down and gently took away the shell. He gave Derrick a wink.

"There's some the sea keeps safe," he said. "And some it just keeps."

With a deep sigh, he stretched out his arms and lifted his furrowed face to the sun.

"It's a fine day for a swim," he said.

Holding the conch in one hand and his wooden staff in the other, he waded into the surf. When the water was half way up his broad back, he turned back towards them.

"You should try it!" he bellowed. "The water's divine!"

Then, as he turned back around, a fin sliced the water, and a dolphin's head appeared beside him.

"Flash?" Derrick whispered.

The dolphin's red eye met his, but only for a

moment. Arching its big scarred back, it leaped high into the air, flicking a rainbow spray from its tail.

Then, with a joyful squeal, it plunged back into the water beside the old man, and they both were gone.

After a long silence, Kerri spoke.

"What did you hear in the shell?"

Derrick smiled as he waded into the water.

"There were three voices," he said. "And one of them sounded a lot like Boris."

# LOOK FOR OTHER

# WHAT WOULD WE DO WITHOUT JILL?

Jill is a pretty, bright girl whose mother makes her feel very unsure of herself. Jill's friends all tell her that she has everything going for her and that she should ignore her mother's comments.

But Jill still wants to be like Molly, her best friend. She wishes it so hard that, briefly, she actually turns into Molly! This is when the two girls discover Jill has an incredible ability to morph into anyone she wants to be. That talent soon becomes a matter of critical importance for Jill. Molly and several other classmates attend a classical concert one afternoon. A gang of crooks, looking for hidden loot, takes over the concert hall and holds prisoner the orchestra and the entire audience of adults and kids. But Jill uses her great morphing skills to confuse the would-be killers—and through many clever morphs and some good common sense, Jill is able to save everyone from being killed by the crooks!